Mole AND Shrew
Have Jobs to Do

by Jackie French Koller
illustrated by Anne Reas

A STEPPING STONE BOOK™

Random House 🏠 New York

To Mallory—a true friend of Mole and Shrew

Text copyright © 2001 by Jackie French Koller
Illustrations copyright © 2001 by Anne Reas

www.randomhouse.com/kids

Library of Congress Cataloging-in-Publication Data
Koller, Jackie French.
Mole and Shrew have jobs to do / by Jackie French Koller ; illustrated by Anne Reas.
p. cm. "A Stepping Stone book."
Summary: Best friends Mole and Shrew need money to buy more of their favorite
things, books and seeds, but none of the jobs they try seems quite right for them.
ISBN 0-375-80691-1 (trade) — ISBN 0-375-90691-6 (lib. bdg.)
[1. Work—Fiction. 2. Moles (Animals)—Fiction. 3. Shrews—Fiction.
4. Best friends—Fiction. 5. Friendship—Fiction. 6. Animals—Fiction.]
I. Reas, Anne, ill. II. Title.
PZ7.K833 Mop 2001 [E]—dc21 00-046950

Printed in the United States of America March 2001 10 9 8 7 6 5 4 3 2 1

☀ Contents ☀

* 1 *

A Problem

Mole poked through his books. They spilled from his bookshelves and filled every spare nook and cranny of his house.

"I read that one twice," he mumbled. "Read that one five times. Oh, I love this one, but I know it by heart. Fuss-'n'-stuff! I am definitely in need of some new books."

Mole climbed up on a stepladder. He took his piggy bank from the top shelf and shook it.

Clinkety clink went the bank.

"What a nice sound," said Mole.

He climbed down again and opened the bank. He gave it a shake and out rolled two pennies.

Mole shook the bank once more.

It was silent.

Mole stuck his fingers inside and wiggled them around.

Nothing.

He held the bank up against his eye and peered into the darkness.

Nothing.

Mole counted his pennies again, more slowly this time.

"O-n-e . . . Two-o-o . . . Nuts," Mole grumbled. "Still only two. Where am I going to find a book for two pennies?"

Just then Mole heard Shrew humming to herself out in her garden. "Hmmm," he said, "perhaps Shrew has some money I could borrow."

Out the back door he went and over to Shrew's house.

"Good day, Shrew," he called cheerfully.

Shrew looked up. "Hello, Mole," she said. "How are you today?"

"Not very well, I'm afraid," said Mole. "My books are old."

"Old books are like old friends," said Shrew. "They're comfortable to have around."

"Indeed," said Mole, "but one needs new friends, too, or one can end up in a rut."

"Very true," said Shrew.

"Which brings me to why I'm here," said Mole.

"You want me to be your new friend?" asked Shrew.

"Of course not," said Mole. "You're too old."

"I beg your pardon," said Shrew.

"I mean, we are old friends," said Mole, "so we can't be new friends."

"I suppose that's true," said Shrew.

"And because we're such old friends," Mole went on, "I thought maybe I could borrow—"

"Of course you may," Shrew interrupted. "You don't have to ask, Mole. Go right in and help yourself to any book on my bookshelves."

"Well . . . that's very kind," said Mole, "but . . . I've already read all your books . . . twice. I was actually hoping to borrow some money."

"Money?" said Shrew.

"Yes," said Mole, "so I might buy some new books."

"I see," said Shrew. Then she sighed. "Actually, Mole, I was just thinking that I would like to buy some new flower seeds. I was about to come over and borrow some money from *you*."

"Hmmm," mused Mole. "That *is* a problem." Then he brightened. "I know," he said. "Why don't I borrow some money from you first, and then you can borrow some back from me!"

"That won't work," said Shrew.

"Why not?" asked Mole.

"Because I don't *have* any money in the first place," said Shrew.

"Oh," said Mole.

"Do you know what we need, Mole?" said Shrew.

"Another old friend?" asked Mole.

"No," said Shrew. "We need jobs."

❋ 2 ❋

Help Wanted

Shrew read down through the "help wanted" listings in the newspaper.

"Tree surgeon?"

Mole cringed. "I faint at the sight of sap," he said.

"Night watchman?"

Mole shivered. "Afraid of the dark."

"Bookkeeper?"

"Ah!" said Mole. "I'm very good at keeping books."

"You are?" said Shrew.

"Indeed," said Mole. "I have kept every book anyone has ever given me."

Shrew grinned. "That's not the kind of bookkeeper they're looking for," she said. "They're looking for someone to write numbers in books."

Mole frowned. "You shouldn't write in books," he said. "It ruins them."

"Not *these* kinds of books," said Shrew. "These are books with empty pages, just for writing numbers in."

"Hmmm," said Mole. "I hope nobody gives me any of *those* books."

Shrew turned the page in the paper. "Newspaper carrier?" she said.

Mole perked up.

"They pay you to do that?" he asked.

"Certainly," said Shrew.

"Well, then." Mole grinned broadly. "Our troubles are over. I have been carrying my newspaper in from the front gate for years. Someone must owe me quite a lot of money!"

Shrew smiled and shook her head.

"No, Mole," she said. "They don't pay you to carry your own newspaper. They pay you to carry the papers and give them to others."

"Humph," said Mole. "I knew there had to be a catch."

Shrew knocked on the door of the newspaper office. Muskrat opened it.

"What is it?" he asked gruffly.

"We came about the newspaper carrier jobs," said Shrew.

"Oh, that," said Muskrat. He looked Mole and Shrew up and down. "All right," he said. "I guess you'll do. You can start tomorrow morning at six o'clock sharp. The papers are stacked in the garage out back. There are wagons back there, too. Help yourself to one. But remember, if you ruin any of the newspapers, you'll have to pay for them."

"What a nice fellow," said Mole as he and Shrew walked away. "I've always wanted a wagon."

"I thought he was rather cranky," said Shrew. "Besides, he isn't *giving* us a wagon, Mole. He's just letting us use it to carry the papers."

"I thought *we* were supposed to carry the papers," said Mole.

"We are," said Shrew. "In the wagon."

"Then they should call us newspaper pullers," said Mole, "not newspaper carriers."

Shrew laughed. "Good point, Mole."

❖ 3 ❖

News Blues

Mole yawned on the way to the news-paper office. "Why do we have to get up so early?" he asked.

"So that our neighbors will be able to have their newspapers for breakfast," said Shrew.

Mole scratched his head. "Our neigh-bors like to have their newspapers for breakfast?" he said.

"Of course," said Shrew. "Don't you?"

"I've never tried it," said Mole. "It

sounds rather dry. Do you put milk on it?"

Shrew looked confused.

"Why would you put milk on a newspaper?" she asked.

"Don't ask me," said Mole. "You're the one who likes newspaper for breakfast. I prefer tea and toast."

Shrew giggled. "I'm not talking about *eating* the newspaper, Mole," she said. "I'm talking about getting it *in time* for breakfast so you can read it while you eat."

"Ah," said Mole. "That makes more sense."

They walked around to the back of the newspaper office and chose a wagon. Out came Muskrat.

"You're one minute late," he said, tapping his watch.

"Sorry," said Mole. "I had a rather hard time waking up so early."

"Well, don't let it happen again," snapped Muskrat. "Your route is Huckleberry Lane, down by the lake. Here is a list of your customers. Make sure you count out just the right number of papers."

Shrew took the list and counted the names.

Mole placed a paper in the wagon for each name.

"That's it," said Shrew. "Let's go."

"Remember," Muskrat warned. "You ruin any of those papers, you pay for them."

"You're right, Shrew," whispered Mole as they walked away. "He *is* rather cranky."

When they got to Huckleberry Lane, Shrew picked up a paper.

"I'll roll up each paper and tie it with

twine," she said. "Then you toss it on the doorstep. Like this."

Shrew tossed a paper, and it landed neatly on Fox's doorstep.

"You are very good at this," said Mole.

"It's like playing horseshoes," said Shrew.

"I never was very good at horseshoes," said Mole.

"I'm sure you'll get the hang of it," said Shrew. "Here. Try Rabbit's hole."

Shrew tied up a paper and handed it to Mole. Mole tossed it.

"It went right in!" he cried.

"OUCH!" someone shouted. Rabbit popped up out of his hole. He rubbed his head, then shook his fist at Mole and Shrew.

"Do that again and I'll bop you!" shouted Rabbit.

"Mercy!" said Mole. "I didn't realize this

job could be dangerous!"

"Perhaps it would be best not to aim quite so close," said Shrew. "Try again."

This time Mole aimed for Otter's front door.

SPLASH! Into the lake went the paper.

"Drat," said Mole. "I guess that wasn't close enough."

Turtle poked up out of the pond. He had a soggy mop of newspaper on his head.

"What's this?" grumbled Turtle. "I didn't order the paper."

"Um . . . free trial today," said Mole. "Compliments of me."

"Free?" whispered Shrew. "We'll have to pay for that paper. And we won't have enough for all our customers."

"It's already ruined anyway," said Mole.

"Free, eh?" said Turtle. "Well, you'd better give me another, then. This one is all wet."

Shrew groaned.

Otter opened his front door. "Where's *my* paper?" he asked.

Mole handed over another.

"Mole," whispered Shrew, "at this rate you'll *never* get a new book!"

"I'm sorry," said Mole. "I'll try to be more careful."

When they arrived at Owl's tree house, Shrew handed Mole another paper.

Mole tossed it up, UP, UP. . . .

It went past Owl's door, up to the tippity top of the tree. There it stayed.

"Uh-oh," said Mole.

Suddenly, a mighty wind came up. Newspapers flew out of the wagon!

"Help!" cried Shrew.

"Catch them!" shouted Mole.

Mole and Shrew scurried about, trying to catch the papers.

"It's no use," said Shrew. "The wind is too strong."

BRR . . . UMBLE UMBLE UMBLE.

"Thunder!" cried Mole. "It's starting to rain."

The clouds opened up and rain poured from the sky. And so did newspaper!

Pieces of wet, soggy newspaper landed on rooftops. They dripped from tree branches. They splatted against houses and plopped in the grass.

And then, as quickly as it had begun, the storm ended.

Mole and Shrew stood staring at the awful scene. A piece of newspaper was plastered to Mole's head. Another sagged from Shrew's shoulders.

"You know something, Mole," said Shrew as they pulled the empty wagon back to the office. "I don't think we can *afford* to be newspaper carriers."

☀ 4 ☀

A Sticky Situation

Back at Shrew's house, Mole rubbed his head with a towel.

"Mefr mer fremfer mun," said Shrew.

"What was that?" asked Mole.

Shrew pointed to an ad in the newspaper.

"Mefr mer fremfer mun," she repeated.

"I can't understand you," said Mole. "Talk clearly."

Shrew came over and pulled some bits of wet newspaper out of Mole's ears.

"How's that?" she asked.

"Much better, thank you," said Mole.

"I was saying," said Shrew, "I've found us another job."

"What is it?" asked Mole.

"Paperhangers," said Shrew.

"Oh no," said Mole. "No more papers, please."

"Not *that* kind of paper," said Shrew. "They're talking about *wall*paper."

"Oh," said Mole. "I like wallpaper."

Shrew read on. "Hmmm," she said. "It says, 'Experience necessary.'"

"I have lots of experience," said Mole.

"Really?" said Shrew. "Are you sure?"

"Very sure," said Mole.

"Well, then," said Shrew, "let's go."

Goose opened her door.

"We're the paperhangers," said Shrew.

"Do you have any experience?" Goose asked.

"Lots," said Mole.

"All right, then," said Goose. "I'm on my way to the market. You'll find the paper and tools in the dining room. Please hang the blue in there and the pink in the bedroom."

Mole and Shrew walked into the dining room. On the tables were some rolls of blue and pink paper, a couple of buckets, some brushes, scissors, a ruler, and a box of powdered paste.

Mole picked up a roll of blue paper and looked around.

"I don't see any hooks," he said.

"Hooks for what?" asked Shrew.

"Why, to hang the paper on, of course," said Mole.

"You don't hang it on hooks," said Shrew. "You hang it on the wall."

"Don't be silly," said Mole. "If you try and hang it on the wall without a hook, it will fall down."

Shrew looked at him oddly. "I thought you had experience hanging wallpaper," she said.

"Who said that?" asked Mole.

"You did."

"I did not."

"Yes, you did, Mole. I asked you if you had experience, and you said yes."

"I *do* have experience," said Mole. "I have experience reading, and writing, and cooking, and singing, and—"

"Mole," interrupted Shrew, "I *meant* experience hanging wallpaper."

"Well," said Mole, "you should have said so."

Shrew sighed. "Now what do we do?"

"Are there directions?" suggested Mole.

Shrew unwrapped a roll of wallpaper. Out fell a paper with writing on it. "Why, yes, there are!" she said.

"Well, then," said Mole, "we're in business!"

Shrew read the directions. "We have to cut the paper slightly longer than the wall," she said. "Then we brush the back of it with paste."

"Where's the paste?" asked Mole.

"In this box," said Shrew. "It says to measure some into the bucket, like this. Now I have to mix it with water. I'll go do that while you cut the paper."

"Very good," said Mole.

He measured the wall and cut the paper. Then he laid it facedown on the table.

Shrew came back in with the paste. She brushed some on the back of the paper. Together, Mole and Shrew carried the piece of wallpaper over and pasted it on the wall. Mole brushed it flat while Shrew trimmed off the edges.

They stood back and admired their work.

"That was easy," said Mole.

"Yes, it was," said Shrew. "Do you think you can handle this room alone while I go do the bedroom?"

"No problem," said Mole.

Shrew carried her tools and the pink paper back to the bedroom.

Mole measured another piece of paper. He pasted the back of it and carried it over to the wall. Just as he was pasting it up—

FLLLOPF!

The piece he and Shrew had just hung

came loose and fell on the floor.

"Nuts," mumbled Mole. He went over and put the paper back up on the wall. He smoothed it with his brush again.

FLLLOPF!

Down fell the other piece.
Mole pasted that one up again.

FLLLOPF! FLLLOPF!

Down fell both pieces at once!
"Hmmm," said Mole. "Perhaps Shrew made the paste too thin."

Mole carried the two pieces of wallpaper back to the table. He dumped more powdered paste into the bucket. He stirred until he could barely move his stick.

"That ought to do it," he said.

Mole took his brush and stuck it into the paste. Then—*thmuck!*—he pulled it out again. He blobbed paste all over the paper. Then he reached to pick it up.

SHWICK!

Mole's hand got stuck.

"Oh my," said Mole. He shook his hand and . . .

SHWICK!

His arm got stuck.

"Dear me," said Mole. He shook his arm and . . .

SHWICK!

His head got stuck.

"Heavens!" grumbled Mole. He grabbed a chair and . . .

SHWICK!

The chair got stuck.

"Fuss-'n'-stuff," mumbled Mole. He

jumped up and down and . . .

THUNK!

His foot kicked over the bucket and . . .

SHWICK!

The rug stuck to his foot!

"Oh drat, drat, drat!" cried Mole.

He twisted and turned and hopped and . . .

Soon there was a huge ball of stuck-up stuff in the middle of the room.

"Phoo," came a muffled voice from inside the ball. "Phoo!"

But Shrew was way back in the bedroom.

Just then Goose came home. She walked into the room.

"Aaagh!" she screamed.

Shrew came running. "What is it?" she

cried. Then she saw the ball. "My good-ness!" she shrieked.

Shrew grabbed a corner of the rug and started to pull. She pulled and pulled until out rolled Mole, covered in paper. Shrew tore a hole in the paper so Mole could talk.

"Shrew," said Mole, "I don't think paper of any kind agrees with me."

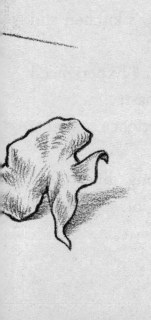

☀5☀

Just Wait!

After a good night's sleep and a hearty breakfast, Mole and Shrew were ready to try again. They sat in Shrew's kitchen and read the paper.

"Here's one," said Mole. "'Experienced pastry chef wanted.' I *love* pastry!"

"Have you any experience *making* pastry?" asked Shrew.

"No," said Mole, patting his round tummy. "But I have *lots* of experience eating it."

"That's *not* the kind of experience they're looking for," said Shrew.

Mole sighed and looked at the paper again. "Heavens!" he cried suddenly.

"What?" asked Shrew.

Mole looked up with wide eyes. "It says, 'Head cook wanted.' Who would want to cook heads?"

Shrew giggled. "They don't want someone to cook heads. They want someone to be the boss of all their other cooks."

Mole shook his head. "Then why don't they say, 'Boss cook wanted'?" he asked.

Shrew rolled her eyes. "Keep reading, Mole," she said.

"'Wait staff'?" said Mole.

"Hmmm," said Shrew. "We could wait."

"Wait for what?" asked Mole.

"Wait on tables, in a restaurant," said Shrew.

"If I have to wait, I'd rather sit in a chair than on a table," said Mole.

Shrew giggled again. "No, Mole," she said. "Waiting on tables means serving people their food."

"I could do that!" said Mole.

Mole and Shrew walked through the door of Owl's Hickory Nut Café. "We called about the waiting jobs," said Shrew to Owl.

"Yes, yes!" said Owl. "You're just in time for the lunch-hour rush. Come with me, please."

Owl took them back into the kitchen and gave them each an apron to put on, a small pad of paper, and a pen. "Hurry," he said. "The customers are waiting."

Owl bustled back out into the dining room, and Mole turned to Shrew. "If the customers are waiting, why do they need us?" he whispered.

Shrew shook her head. "The customers are waiting for *us* to wait on *them*," she said.

"What a confusing business," said Mole.

Shrew tied her apron around her waist.

"Just go out and start taking orders," she said.

Mole tied his apron on, too. Then he followed Shrew into the dining room. It was filled with hungry customers.

Shrew hurried right over to a table.

Mole stood and looked around.

Shrew ran to another table.

Mole looked around some more.

Shrew rushed by. "What are you waiting for?" she asked shortly.

"To earn money to buy books, of course," said Mole.

"No," said Shrew. "I mean, why aren't you taking orders?"

"I'm *waiting* for orders," said Mole, "but nobody is giving me any."

"Mole!" shouted Owl. "What are you waiting for?"

"To earn money to buy books," replied Mole.

"Well, get hopping!" shouted Owl.

"Is that an order?" asked Mole.

"Yes, that's an order!" yelled Owl.

"All right," said Mole. He started hopping around.

"What are you doing?" cried Owl.

"Taking orders," said Mole.

"For heaven's sake, Mole, will you please stand still!" wailed Owl.

Mole stopped hopping. "Why don't you

decide what you want?" he told Owl.

"I want you to take orders!" repeated Owl. "Now start with that table over there and hop to it!"

Mole sighed. He hopped to the table.

"Don't you know how to walk?" cried Owl.

"Of course I know how to walk," said Mole.

"Then walk!" said Owl.

Mole started walking.

"Where are you going now?" cried Owl.

"I don't know," said Mole. "Where do you want me to go?"

"I want you to march right back to that table!"

Mole turned and started marching.

"I said *walk*!" boomed Owl.

"You said *march*!" snapped Mole.

Owl folded his wings over his chest.

"That's just about enough of your impudence!" he said. "One more word and you're fired!"

Mole stood silently in the middle of the room. He was feeling very confused.

Over came Shrew. "Is there something wrong?" she asked.

Owl shook his head. "Your friend is a lunkhead!" he bellowed.

Shrew frowned.

Mole leaned over to whisper in her ear. "What is a lunkhead?" he asked.

"It's a person who is much too smart to work in this restaurant," said Shrew. "Come along, Mole. We have better things to do."

6

Ducky Day!

The next morning, Mole and Shrew looked through the paper once again.

"I'm afraid we're running out of jobs, Mole," said Shrew.

Mole sighed. "There must be *some* business we're suited for," he said.

"I'm sure there is, Mole," said Shrew. "We'll just keep looking. Come on. Let's take a walk to cheer ourselves up."

Mole and Shrew strolled through town. They passed Gopher, directing traffic. They passed Rat, delivering milk. They passed Frog, selling fruit from a cart.

"Everyone has jobs but us," Mole grumbled.

"Something is *bound* to turn up," Shrew assured him.

Suddenly, Mole perked up.

"I do believe you're right, Shrew!" he said. "Look at that sign."

They were passing a little white house with a yard full of toys.

Ducky Day Care

said the sign. Then underneath, a smaller sign said

Help Wanted—Apply Within

Shrew clapped her hands. "I would love to help take care of children," she said.

"Well, then," said Mole, "let's go in!"

Mole and Shrew pushed the door open and stepped into the house. Children were running everywhere. Toys sailed through the air. A small turtle on a tricycle ran right over Mole's toe!

"Ouch!" said Mole. "I think this job might be too dangerous!"

"Don't be silly," said Shrew. "They're just children."

A little warthog toddled by.

"Hello there," said Shrew. "What's your name?"

"Piglet," said the little warthog.

"Can you tell me where your teacher is, Piglet?" Shrew asked.

Piglet pointed to an open door at the side of the room. Mole and Shrew could see cribs beyond and hear babies crying.

"HELLO," Shrew called over the din. "HELLO!"

Duck appeared in the doorway. She had a screaming baby squirrel in her arms. "Oh, hello!" she shouted. "I was just changing the babies. Come in."

Mole bent close to Shrew. "I don't think she should change those babies," he said. "I'll bet their parents like them just the way they are."

Shrew laughed. "She's changing their *diapers*, Mole," she explained.

Mole's eyes popped. *"Diapers?"* he said. "You don't think *we'll* have to change diapers, do you?"

Shrew shrugged. "We'll see."

Shrew pulled Mole over to Duck.

"We saw your sign," Shrew told Duck. "Are you still looking for help?"

"Sakes, yes!" said Duck. "When could you start?"

"Right now," said Shrew.

"Great. You're both hired," said Duck. "Now, which one of you would like to help me diaper and feed the babies?"

"Shrew would," Mole said quickly.

"All right," said Duck. "Then you can read the older children a story, Mole. Come, I'll introduce you."

"A story!" Mole grinned. "I think I am going to like this job!"

Duck handed the baby squirrel to

Shrew. Then she gathered the older children into a circle.

"This is Mole," said Duck. "He's going to read to you."

"Yay!" The children clapped.

"Meet Gosling, Piglet, Kit, Cub, Duckling, and Fawn," Duck told Mole. "They love stories. Just choose a book from the bookshelves. I'll be in the nursery if you need me."

Mole nodded and went over to the bookshelves.

"Ah." He pulled out a worn copy of *Where the Tame Things Are*. "Here is one that Mother Mole used to read to me!" he said.

Mole sat down next to the children. "'The night Wolf wore his Max suit . . . ,'" he began.

The children listened quietly as Mole

read. They watched as he turned the pages.

I do *like this job*, Mole thought to himself.

From the other room Mole could still hear babies crying. After a while, Shrew poked her head out. She was rocking a baby bunny in her arms.

"How are things out here?" she asked.

"Very fine," said Mole. "How are things in there?"

"Damp," said Shrew, "and noisy." Then she disappeared again.

When Mole finished reading the story, he closed the book and put it in his lap.

"Now," he said, "does anyone have any questions?"

Gosling raised her wing.

"Yes?" said Mole.

"Did you ever pee your pants?" asked Gosling.

"Wh-what?" stammered Mole.

"I peed my pants yesterday," Gosling went on. "It ran down my leg and onto the floor, and Kit stepped in it."

"Oh my!" Mole blushed. "That's too bad. I mean, I'm sure you didn't mean to, but . . ."

Cub's hand shot up.

"Yes?" said Mole, happy to change the subject.

"Did you ever poop your pants?" asked Cub.

"What? My word! Of course not," said Mole.

"Not even when you were a baby?" asked Piglet.

"Well, maybe when I was a baby," said Mole. "Babies do that sort of thing . . ."

"My baby sister pooped in the pond," Duckling shouted out, "and it floated!"

"My brother pooped . . . ," Kit began.

Harrumph! Mole interrupted. "I'm sure that's all very interesting, but does anyone *else* have a question?"

A dozen hands shot up.

"A question that is *not* about pee or poop," Mole added.

All the hands went down. Then, slowly, Fawn's went up again.

Mole brightened. "Yes, Fawn," he said. "What would you like to ask?"

"Did you ever throw up?" asked Fawn.

✲ 7 ✲

Dwiddle. Dwiddle. Dwiddle.

"Mole," said Duck, "do you think you can give the children their painting lesson? I have to run out for more diapers."

"Certainly," said Mole. "I'm a very good painter."

"Excellent," said Duck. "The paints are in the cupboard under the sink."

Mole went over and peeked into the nursery. Shrew was trying to give bottles to a baby beaver and a baby badger. A crying turtle tugged on her skirt. Shrew looked very tired.

"How are you doing?" Mole asked.

Shrew sighed. "Caring for children is quite a challenge," she said.

"It certainly is," Mole agreed. A ball bounced off his head. "Better get back to work," he said.

Mole went over to the sink and opened the paint cupboard.

"My, what a nice selection of colors," he said.

He handed a jar to each child. Then he gave each child a brush. He looked around the room. "There's a nice big wall," he said. "Let's start there."

"Yay!" screamed the children.

They ran over and started splattering paint all over the wall.

"This is boring," said Cub. "I want to make a flower."

"I'm afraid you can't *make* a flower," said Mole kindly. "A flower is a living thing. Only

51

Mother Nature can make a flower."

"I want to make fish," said Fawn.

"I'm afraid a fish is a living thing, too," said Mole.

"I want to make a poop," said Gosling.

"No more poop talk," said Mole.

"But I have to," cried Gosling. She started jumping around in a circle. "I have to right *now*!"

"Oh. *OH!*" said Mole. "Well, run along, then. Hurry!"

Gosling rushed to the bathroom.

"Poop, poop," said Piglet. The other children all giggled.

"No more saying *poop*," Mole said firmly.

"But what if we have to?" asked Duckling.

Mole thought for a moment. "Say *dwiddle* instead, and I'll know what you mean."

"*Dwiddle*," said Cub. "I have to *dwiddle*."

"You do?" asked Mole.

"No." Cub giggled. "I just like to say it. *Dwiddle. Dwiddle. Dwiddle.*"

"*Dwiddle. Dwiddle. Dwiddle*," sang the other children.

Mole sighed.

"Can I say *throw-up*?" asked Kit.

"No," said Mole.

"Dwiddle. Dwiddle. Dwiddle," the children sang more loudly.

"But what if—" Kit began.

"Dwiddle. Dwiddle. Dwiddle," the others chanted.

"Enough!" Mole shouted. "No more pee, no more poop, no more dwiddle, no more throw-up. From now on you are to say nothing! Do you understand?"

BLECH! went Kit. He threw up on Mole's foot.

"Aaagh!" cried Mole. "What is that?"

"Nothing," said Kit.

✹ 8 ✹

Too Much of a Good Thing

Mole and Shrew trudged slowly home.

"I think it was very rude of Duck to fire us," said Shrew.

"I agree," said Mole. "Just because you fell asleep."

"Well, she did seem annoyed about the wall, too," said Shrew.

Mole snorted. "If she wanted them to paint on paper, she should have said so."

"I was getting rather tired of pee and poop anyway," said Shrew.

"Me too!" agreed Mole.

Mole was exhausted when he got home. He fell into a chair and picked up one of his favorite books. He began to read. He read and read. Soon he felt better.

When Shrew got home, she went out to her garden to relax.

"These daisies are getting overgrown," she said to herself, "and the brown-eyed Susans are getting very thick. I think it's time to do a bit of thinning."

Shrew got out her wheelbarrow. Then she went to her potting shed and filled it with pots. Back to the garden she went. Before long she had dozens of pots filled with flowers of all kinds.

"Now, what to do with these?" she wondered. "Maybe Mole could use them."

Shrew went over to Mole's house.

"Hello, Shrew," said Mole when he came to the door. "What have you there?"

"I've been thinning out my garden," she said. "I'm making room for the new seeds I'm going to get once we find a way to earn money."

Mole nodded. "That makes sense. Perhaps I should clean out some of my bookshelves, too."

Shrew peeked around Mole. "Goodness," she said. "Your books have been piling up, haven't they?"

"Yes." Mole nodded. "There's hardly room for me anymore."

Shrew chuckled. "I was wondering if you want any of these plants I've been thinning out," she said.

Mole looked at Shrew's wheelbarrow. "That's very kind," he said. "But I'm afraid my garden is a bit overgrown, too."

Shrew looked at Mole's yard. "Oh my, you're right," she said. "Those lilies are positively taking over. And look at your mums! I'll give you a hand once I figure out what to do with all these extras of mine."

"Perhaps you should set up a little table by the road and sell them," said Mole. "They're quite lovely."

"Why, that's an *excellent* idea!" said Shrew.

"I have an extra table," said Mole. "Would you like to borrow it?"

"That would be wonderful," said Shrew.

"Come in, then," said Mole, "and we'll carry it out together."

Shrew followed Mole into his house. There were books everywhere—on the shelves, on the tables, on the chairs, in piles on the floor. Mole's spare table was piled high with books, too.

"Mole," said Shrew, "you really *must* do something about all these books."

"I know," said Mole. "But they are hard to part with."

"I have an idea," said Shrew. "Why don't you sell some books, too?"

"I don't know," said Mole. "I'm not sure I could sell my books."

"Wouldn't it make you feel good to know that others were getting a chance to read them?" asked Shrew.

"Yes," said Mole. "That would be rather nice."

"Well, why not try it, then?" asked Shrew.

"No," said Mole. "I just don't think I could." He leaned back against the table.

Thump!

A pile of books went tumbling sideways.

BUMP!

They crashed into another stack on the chair.

Clunk!

That stack toppled over and bumped into a floor lamp.

SMASH!

The lamp went crashing through Mole's front window.

Mole scratched his head. "Hmmm," he said. "On second thought, maybe I *could* part with a few."

✺9✺

Petals & Pages!

A small crowd gathered in front of Mole and Shrew's table.

"What is that pretty purple flower?" asked Lizard.

"It's a primrose," said Shrew. "Isn't it lovely?"

"It is," said Lizard. "Will it bloom year after year?"

"Yes, it will," said Shrew. "Just be sure and plant it in a sunny spot."

"Do you have anything that likes the

shade?" asked Hedgehog.

"Certainly," said Shrew. "These lilies do well in the shade, and so do coral bells."

"I'll take one of each, then," said Hedgehog.

Rabbit thumbed through Mole's books. He held up one titled *Peg-Leg Possum*. "Have you read this one?" he asked.

"Three times," said Mole.

"Is it any good?" asked Rabbit.

"Of course it's good," said Mole indignantly. "Do you think I'd read it three times if it weren't?"

"Maybe. Maybe not," said Rabbit. "What is it about?"

"It's a pirate adventure," said Mole.

Rabbit's eyes widened. "That *does* sound interesting," he said.

"Have you got any mysteries?" asked Tortoise.

"Yes, lots!" said Mole. He pulled out a book called *The Missing Marmoset*. "You won't be able to put this one down!"

"I think I *will* take this one," said Rabbit.

"Excellent," said Mole. "Do come back and tell me how you like it."

"How about romances?" asked Heron, batting her eyes. "I just *love* a good romance."

"I have just the thing!" said Mole. "It's in the house. I'll run right in and get it."

Mole came out carrying a book called *In Love with a Loon*.

The crowd was even larger. Shrew's flowers were selling like hotcakes. More folks were standing with books in hand, clamoring for Mole's advice.

"Do you have any books on bread?" asked Otter.

Mole stopped and stared. "I beg your

pardon?" he said.

"I would like a book on bread," said Otter.

Mole frowned. "This isn't a sandwich shop," he said. "And besides, that's disgusting. What kind of person eats books?"

"Eats books?" said Otter. "What are you talking about?"

"Well, why else would you want a book on bread?" asked Mole.

Otter started to laugh. "I'm sorry," he said. "I didn't mean a book *on* bread. I meant a book about *baking* bread. I want to learn how to make it."

"Oh!" cried Mole with a sigh of relief. "Well, why didn't you say so? I have just the book. *Baking with Badger*."

"Why, thank you," said Otter. "You certainly are good at your job."

"My job?" repeated Mole.

"Yes," said Otter. "And aren't you lucky to be able to make money doing something you love?"

Mole stared at Otter for a long moment. Then he turned and watched Shrew, happily chatting with her customers. He started to grin.

"Yes, Otter, I am," he said. "Very lucky indeed! Excuse me a moment, will you?"

Mole hurried back into his house. He got a big piece of paper, a crayon, and some tape.

"What have you got there, Mole?" asked Shrew when he returned.

Mole printed something on the paper, then went around front and taped it to the table. "Come see," he said.

Shrew went and looked at the sign.

Petals & Pages

it said in large letters. Then underneath, Mole had written

MOLE AND SHREW'S

BOOK and Flower Shop

Mole beamed. "Don't you see, Shrew?" he said. "We're in business!"

Shrew smiled, too. "Why, so we are!" she cried. "And what a clever name, Mole."

Mole blushed. "Thank you," he said. "My mother gave it to me. It was my father's name, and my grandfather's, too. Come to think of it, it was my mother's name, too, and my aunt Mole's, and . . ."

Shrew chuckled. "Mole," she said, "I meant, what a clever name you thought up for our shop."

"Yes, it is, isn't it?" said Mole. He gazed

69

proudly at his Petals & Pages sign. "Perhaps we should celebrate our new business, Shrew," he said.

"Indeed we should!" said Shrew. Then she looked at the crowd of customers milling around their table. "But not right now, Mole. Right now, you and I have jobs to do!"